BEASTQUEST

→∘ BOOK THREE ∘←

CYPHER
THE MOUNTAIN GIANT

ADAM BLADE

ILLUSTRATED BY EZRA TUCKER

SCHOLASTIC INC.

New York Toronto London Auckland Sydney
Mexico City New Delhi Hong Kong Buenos Aires

With thanks to Kyle and Tyrell,
my family

ISBN-13: 978-0-545-09434-4
ISBN-10: 0-545-09434-8

12 11 10 9 8 7 6 5 4 3 2 1   8 9 10 11 12 13/0

Printed in the U.S.A.   40

First Book Club paperback printing, September 2008

Designed by Tim Hall

Reader,

Welcome to Avantia. I am Aduro — a good wizard residing in the palace of King Hugo. You join us at a difficult time. Let me explain. . . .

It is laid down in the Ancient Scripts that the peaceful kingdom of Avantia would one day be plunged into danger by the evil wizard, Malvel.

That time has come.

Under Malvel's evil spell, six Beasts — fire dragon, sea serpent, mountain giant, night horse, ice beast, and winged flame — run wild and destroy the land they once protected.

The kingdom is in great danger.

The Scripts also predict an unlikely hero. They say that a boy shall take up the Quest to free the beasts and save the kingdom.

We hope this young boy will take up the Quest. Will you join us as we wait and watch?

Avantia salutes you,
Aduro

↦ PROLOGUE ↤

THE CARAVAN MOVED SLOWLY ALONG THE HIGH mountain road. As the slope became steeper, the horses struggled to pull the wagons loaded with goods and supplies.

"How much longer?" a boy in the first wagon asked impatiently.

His father looked ahead at the rock-strewn road that snaked its way up the mountainside. "Once we get to the pass, it's not much farther, Jack," he said, pointing to a ridge in the distance.

Jack looked toward the ridge. Above it, dark clouds were beginning to gather. They cast long shadows down the mountainside, and the boy felt the air cool as the sun disappeared behind the clouds.

When the caravan rounded a bend in the road, they were hit by a fierce mountain wind. Jack shivered with cold as he pulled his coat tighter.

"We'd better hurry if we're going to beat this storm," Jack's father called to the other men, his voice almost lost in the wind. "We don't want to get stuck and freeze to death."

The caravan pushed on. The wind gained in strength and was now screaming through the trees. Then, as the caravan came to another bend in the road, a thunderous crashing echoed through the valley.

Startled, Jack glanced up at the ridge. There, standing as tall as the trees, was a giant. He held a huge boulder between his clawed hands, and only had one, large eye in the middle of his forehead. Right now, that eye was fixed on Jack and the caravan.

"Look! Over there!" Jack yelled to his father, pointing toward the nearest peak.

"What is it, Jack?" the man asked, keeping his eyes on the trail ahead.

"I saw — I saw — "

But before Jack could finish his sentence, the ground began to shake. The caravan halted and the men looked around in confusion.

They could hear a deep rumbling sound. Then, in the distance, there was a loud crack of splintering wood, as if trees were being snapped in half.

"What's happening, Dad?" Jack asked with panic in his voice.

His father looked toward the ridgeline and then back at Jack. "I don't know, son," he said.

It was the first time Jack had seen fear in his father's eyes, and it sent shivers down his spine.

As they stood there, trapped, the crashing grew louder — and nearer. The ground trembled so violently beneath their feet that it was hard to stand. The horses reared up, trying to break free of their harnesses.

A wagon broke from its hitch and began to slide back down the road, its contents spilling everywhere. Men dove out of the way as the heavy barrels tumbled toward them. Everywhere there was chaos. Then, just in front of them, a huge boulder tore through the trees and across the narrow mountain road, nearly hitting Jack and his father.

"Run! Run for your lives!"

CHAPTER ONE

A NEW ADVENTURE

AT THE CREST OF THE FOOTHILLS, TOM AND Elenna came to a fork in the road. The road to the east continued along the ridgeline toward the farms of Avantia. The road to the north disappeared into the mountains.

Tom knew which one they needed to take to find the next Beast.

But Elenna hesitated. The towering mountains were wrapped in dark, ominous clouds, and Tom could sense his friend's nervousness. He knew this was going to be even more dangerous than the last mission.

"Don't worry, Elenna. We'll be okay," Tom said.

Then, smiling, he added, "I mean, I've got you and the mutt for protection, don't I?"

"Thank you *very* much!" Elenna beckoned her pet wolf, Silver, who was sniffing some bushes nearby. "Come on, boy — time to teach our friend a lesson in manners!"

Silver shot to her side like a sleek gray arrow. Elenna pointed at Tom and the wolf playfully nipped at his heels as they set out on the road to the north.

"*Ow!*" Tom cried.

"Take it back!" Elenna demanded.

"All right! All right! I take it back!" Tom exclaimed, holding up his shield as Silver leaped up at him. "I'll never call him a mutt again!"

Elenna gave a short whistle. Silver immediately left Tom and trotted to her side. Elenna shot Tom a sideways look.

Tom smiled and nodded. They were in this together.

Before he'd met Elenna, Tom had been chosen by King Hugo and his royal advisor, the wizard Aduro, to go on a quest. He was to save the kingdom of Avantia from the Beasts, who were under the evil spell of the Dark Wizard Malvel. Before the Quest, Tom used to think the Beasts only existed in legend. But now that he had fought two of them himself, he knew just how real they were — and how deadly they could be.

Ever since Malvel had gained control of the Beasts through his dark magic, they had been carrying out acts of terror and destruction. Tom's mission was to stop them. He had to break Malvel's hold over the Beasts.

So far, Tom had faced the fiery wrath of Ferno the Fire Dragon, and the horror of Sepron, a monstrous sea serpent. He and Elenna had only survived by working together. Now Aduro had warned them that a new danger lurked in the mountains of the North.

Giant danger.

Tom brought Storm to a halt and reached into one of the horse's saddlebags. "Let's check that we're going the right way." He jumped down and unrolled the magic map that Aduro had given him. Trees and hills and mountains rose up from the old parchment paper, standing as tall as Tom's thumbnail. Near a hillside, a part of the path was glowing.

"That's where we are now," Elenna said, as Storm rested his muzzle on Tom's shoulder. "Another day's ride and we should reach Colton."

Of all the towns nestled among the peaks of the northern mountains, Colton was the biggest. Tom looked at the drawing of the town on the map. It was surrounded by five mountains that rose up on all sides, jagged and forbidding. The road leading to the town was long and winding, and in one part it looked as if it was blocked. This meant they would have to find a way around. Tom had never tried to climb a mountain before and wondered if it would be as steep and dangerous as he imagined.

"We'd better make camp soon," Tom said. "We're going to need all our energy to get up that mountain pass tomorrow."

Elenna mounted Storm and Tom led the way with Silver. As they picked their way up the hillside, the mountains towered all around them.

When they reached the top of the hill and paused to catch their breath, they couldn't believe what lay before them. Mountains stretched as far as they could see. Dark shadows filled their cracks and gullies, while the peaks seemed to glow in the late afternoon sun. Like rows of sharp teeth, the mountains stood out against the deep blue sky. In the distance, near where Colton would be, dark clouds were beginning to gather.

"It's beautiful," said Elenna. Tom nodded. He'd seen many things on his Quest so far, but nothing as breathtaking as this. He swallowed hard.

As they were getting ready to continue on their way, they noticed a raggedy group of men coming down the trail toward them. Tom gripped his sword.

One of the men called out a greeting as the group drew nearer. Tom could make out that one of them was carrying a young boy over his shoulder.

When the group reached them, Tom and Elenna could see that the men were traders. They looked dirty and tired, and the boy appeared to be injured, his head wrapped in a bloody strip of cloth.

"Can you help us?" the man carrying the boy asked desperately. "Do you have any water? All our supplies were destroyed."

Tom passed him his water canteen. "What happened?"

"We were part of a trading caravan, bringing supplies to the town of Colton," the man explained. "And then the ground started to shake and a rockslide came down the side of the mountain — we were lucky to survive."

"What triggered it?" asked Elenna.

"We don't know. The mountains are usually very stable. But the weather was unusual and —"

"The giant —" sputtered the injured boy. "There was a giant —"

Tom and Elenna exchanged glances.

"Don't mind the boy," one of the men said quietly. "He got a bump on his head."

"No, I saw it. I swear," said the boy. In a trembling voice, he described the violent shaking and the sound of trees being snapped as boulders tore down the mountainside.

When the boy had finished, one of the men said grimly, "I hope you two aren't going into the mountains."

"I'm afraid we are," said Tom.

The men looked at each other, concern on their

faces. "The mountains are a dangerous place, even in the best conditions," the leader warned. "The main route is blocked now and the weather's been bad for weeks. I'd turn back."

"We don't have a choice," Tom said bravely.

The trader seemed to understand. "Well, if you must go, take this." He handed Tom a short length of rope. "It's not much, but it's all I have. It may come in handy."

It was now growing late and the sun was close to setting.

"You'd better get going," said the kindly trader. "There's a good place to make camp not too far north from here."

"Thank you," said Tom and Elenna. They gave the traders some more of their water and all the food they could spare, then bid them good-bye.

Tom and Elenna took one last look at the mountains. Tom wondered if something so beautiful could be as dangerous as the traders had warned.

Elenna mounted Storm and the four of them made their way down the other side of the hill. On their way down, the sky grew dark and it began to drizzle.

"We'd better hurry up and make camp!" Elenna cried out. "We're going to get soaked."

At the bottom of the hill, they crossed a small stream in the gully. The mountain water was crystal clear and ice cold.

Tom knew it would be dangerous to sleep in the gully. If it kept raining, the stream might overflow and their camp would end up underwater. He scanned the next hill and spotted an outcropping of rock that would provide good shelter for the night.

As they began their way up the next hill, Silver tensed and started to growl.

"What is it, boy?" Tom crouched beside the

wolf. He looked all around, but the whole area was deserted.

Elenna shivered. "Let's get going."

They set off again, picking a path between the trees scattered along the hillside.

Silver growled again. Storm nickered nervously, his ears pricked up straight as his hooves skidded on the wet grass.

Storm lunged forward and then stopped dead, all four hooves planted firmly on the ground. "Come on, Storm," Elenna said, touching her heels to his sides. "It's all right. . . ." She broke off with a gasp. Storm was slowly moving down the hillside, even though he was standing still. "Tom!" Elenna cried as a rumbling noise started up. Storm started to slide more quickly. "The ground's not safe!"

"Get off Storm!" Tom yelled as the horse fought to keep his balance. Elenna jumped, just as Storm's hind legs slipped from under him. With a crash, the horse fell heavily onto his side. His hooves sent great clods of mud flying into the air and Elenna fell to the ground with a cry.

"Storm! Elenna!" Tom yelled, his voice filled with panic.

Elenna's eyes were wide in horror as she pointed up the hill, past Tom.

"Mudslide!" she screamed.

CHAPTER TWO

SWEPT AWAY

TOM SPUN AROUND. HE LOOKED IN SHOCK AS A sludgy torrent of mud surged down the hill toward them. It was as if the ground was *melting*. . . .

With a terrified snort, Storm struggled back to his feet, his coat caked with mud. Silver tugged at Elenna's sleeve, trying to drag her to safety. Tom began to carefully make his way back down the hill to his companions.

But with a lurch, the ground gave way beneath him. Tom cried out as he was sucked into the thick, swirling muck. His back scraped over roots as he was swept down the hillside. Tom saw the terror in Elenna's face as he rushed toward her in a mass of dark mud. As the thick wave hit her, Elenna reached for Tom's hand. She caught hold of it for a moment, but it was soon wrenched away. Tom reached out for her again but his fingers closed on grass and mud.

"Elenna!" he yelled.

Storm kicked wildly as he tried to escape. Tom threw himself to one side to avoid the horse's thrashing hooves. Elenna was swept away from Tom and her head disappeared under the mud.

"I can't breathe!" she yelled, fighting her way to the surface.

"Reach out to your right!" Tom shouted. "Grab hold of Storm's reins!"

Blindly, Elenna reached out and managed to grab them. "Where's Silver?" she yelled.

As the torrent tossed Tom around, he caught a glimpse of the hillside above them — and it wasn't good. The entire top half seemed to be collapsing behind them. Trees and bushes were tumbling into the waves of mud that were furiously ripping them from the ground. With a rush of relief, Tom saw the wolf racing along beside them on firmer ground, howling furiously. "Get away, Silver!" Tom shouted. "There's nothing you can do to help us!"

Tom reached out for something solid — something to grab a hold of — anything! His hand scraped against a boulder and he managed to find a fingerhold. He fought to hang on as mud and debris rushed past him. Tom wasn't sure how long he could keep his grip on the wet rock.

Storm was swept farther down the hill with Elenna dragging behind, clinging to his reins. The horse's huge flank slammed into a few tall, sturdy trees and Elenna crashed into his side. The trees were keeping both of them from being swept away — for now, at least.

"Don't let go of Storm's reins, Elenna!" Tom shouted above the roar.

Elenna gritted her teeth as she held on tight. Snorting in fear, Storm struggled to haul himself upright, leaning heavily against the trees.

Exhausted, Tom tried to pull himself up the side of the boulder. The ground was shaking, the black mud was sucking at his ankles, but with all his strength he kept pulling himself upward. Just a little farther . . .

But it was too late. With Elenna's screams echoing in his ears, Tom braced himself as another surge of mud hit them.

He squeezed his eyes shut as the gritty wave tumbled over him. He was almost ripped from the boulder by the force of it. It was all he could do to drag a breath into his lungs as the mud and debris tore at his clothes and grazed his skin.

With a final burst of strength, Tom reached for the top of the boulder. He let out a loud yell as he clawed to the top. His voice echoed above the angry churning of the mud. He wasn't going to be defeated!

CHAPTER THREE

AFTERMATH

THE MUD KEPT COMING, PULLING FIERCELY AT Tom's legs. He could hear his knuckles pop as he strained to keep his grip on the slippery boulder. Tom thrashed his legs, trying to locate a foothold. He found one just to his right. As he gained his footing, it took some of the strain off his fingers.

With his foot in place, Tom took a step up, and began clambering to the top of the boulder. His tired muscles trembled as he watched the mudslide become a slow ooze of debris.

Once he was sure the danger was past, he eased himself down to the soggy ground. Tom felt a rush of panic as he looked for Elenna. All around him the hillside was destroyed. Only a few trees were left standing in the muddy wasteland. He wiped the mud from his eyes and walked in circles, looking for his friends.

"Tom!" Elenna yelled. She was waist deep in mud, still holding tightly to Storm's reins. Tom made his way over as they struggled to free themselves from the muck. From the other side of the hill, Silver padded his way over to his muddy companions.

The slide had slowed to a crawl. Tom was exhausted. It felt like he was wearing a suit of armor; even the smallest movements seemed to take all his strength. Storm walked carefully to meet him. Shivering with cold, Tom gratefully wrapped his arms around Storm's neck, sinking his hands into the horse's thick, muddy mane. Tom let go of the horse as Elenna approached.

"I was so scared," said Elenna, hugging Tom tight. "I thought we were going to be killed."

"Me, too," gasped Tom. His legs felt wobbly and he leaned against Storm for support.

"You're freezing," said Elenna.

Tom saw that Elenna was shivering, too, and her face was pale. This wasn't the time to show weakness. He had to be strong. "I'm all right," he said. "I'll warm up once we get moving."

Elenna nodded. "Good idea. Let's get to safer ground and then make camp."

The four of them hiked cautiously toward the outcropping of rock Tom had spotted earlier. The rain had stopped, but the ground was still thick with mud. Each step took great effort as they made their way up.

By the time they reached the rocks, the sun had set. The air had grown colder and it was too dark to see. Guided only by starlight, Tom and Elenna found a cave in the rock wall.

"Let's make camp in here," Tom suggested. He

could tell from the look on Elenna's face that she was scared.

"What if there's another mudslide?" she asked. "We could be trapped inside."

Tom had considered the same thing himself, but he knew they didn't have a choice. It was too cold and dangerous to spend the night without some shelter. They would have to take their chances.

The four of them entered the cave. It smelled damp and echoed with their footsteps. Silver eyed the place suspiciously and sniffed around. Satisfied, he padded over to Elenna and curled up next to her. As Tom laid out his bedroll, he wished they could have a warm fire. He could feel his stomach growling with hunger, but that would have to wait. Before he could suggest they build a fire or cook some dinner, he was overcome with exhaustion and fell asleep.

CHAPTER FOUR

IN THE SHADOW OF THE MOUNTAINS

TOM AND ELENNA AWOKE LATE AS THE SUN shone brightly into the mouth of the cave. Every muscle in Tom's body ached. Rubbing the sleep from his eyes, he looked around at the cave walls. It had been too dark — and he had been too tired — to notice them the night before.

On the walls were drawings made with ancient charcoal. They seemed to be telling a story. Tom recognized what looked like jagged mountains, and simple pictures of men with spears and clubs. On another wall were the same mountains and what looked like an enormous hand. Tom took the key from around his neck and looked back at the drawings on the cave wall. This key had freed Ferno and Sepron — would it free Cypher as well?

As Tom was studying the cave drawings, Elenna woke up. "What are they?" she asked.

"I don't know," said Tom. "But it looks like someone knew about the giant long ago."

"It's late. We should get moving," Elenna said, gathering up her bedroll.

"All right," Tom agreed, tearing his eyes away from the cave's walls. He took hold of Storm's reins and followed Elenna to the mouth of the cave.

They stood blinking in the sunlight. The mudslide had left a thick scar on the landscape, blocking the main trail. To get around it, they would have to follow the muddy scar down into the next valley. Then it was a long climb back up to the other side of the trail. Tom and Elenna walked beside Storm with Silver bounding at their heels.

When they reached the top, they found themselves looking upon a range of mountains stretching toward the horizon.

Elenna gasped. "That's amazing!"

Tom led the way down a path in the shadow of the mountains. The hill was steep, with a cliff on one side. There were lots of loose pebbles and Tom had to pick his way carefully. One wrong step and it would be a very long fall.

Tom looked at his map. Then he looked around. "This is strange," he said. "We should have reached Colton by now. But it's nowhere to be seen."

"Maybe we'll see something from the top of this hill," said Elenna, pointing at the gentle slope in front of them.

They climbed carefully, their feet slipping and sliding in the silt and rubble. Then, suddenly, a loud crack rang out from beneath Storm's hooves. Tom put a hand on Storm's neck and they all froze.

"What was *that*?" Tom asked, crouching down. He quickly cleared away some of the dust. His hands scraped against something — it was a piece of slate, neatly overlapped by others surrounding it.

"Roof tiles," he said, realizing where they were. "Elenna — we're standing on a roof!"

"Then, this isn't a hill at all!" Elenna said. She looked up at the mountainside and the bare face of rock covered in angry cracks. "This is a house that's been buried by a rockslide. It could collapse any minute!"

"Look," said Tom, pointing over to a shape farther up the hill. It was the top of an archway, the gateway to the mountain trade routes. "I think there's a whole street buried under this rubble!"

"Come on, let's get down quickly before we crash right through this roof." Treading as lightly

as they could, Tom and Elenna led Storm and Silver back down the slope.

Using the roof and archway as marker points, they worked out roughly where the street must have been. They made their way over the rocks and rubble until they found a part of town built into the hillside. The rockslide hadn't buried these buildings. The houses were grand and tall with wooden fronts, and the streets were neatly paved with cobblestones. Tom looked around him and whistled.

"Looks like a nice part of town," said Elenna. There weren't any houses like this in Tom's village. But the place was deserted. "I hope everyone got to safety."

Suddenly, Silver looked toward the mountains, sniffing the air. He growled uneasily and started stalking back the way they had come. "What's wrong, boy?" Elenna took hold of his collar, but he strained against her grip. Silver never disobeyed Elenna. She frowned and pointed down the street. "We're going *this* way." She looked at Tom. "What's wrong with him?"

But as she spoke, shouts and the sounds of a commotion came from somewhere close by.

Tom looked at her. "Silver must have sensed trouble."

"Stop, thieves!" someone shouted.

Tom jumped onto Storm and Elenna leaped up behind him. He drew his sword out of one of Storm's saddlebags and pressed his heels against the horse's sides. Storm didn't need telling twice. He bolted off along the cobbled street toward the sounds of trouble.

"Silver isn't following us!" Elenna cried. She pointed after the wolf, who was running in the opposite direction.

"We'll go back for him later," Tom told her. Storm thundered over the cobblestones, making it difficult for them to hold on. "Right now, someone needs our help."

They turned into a narrow back alley. Three men with bulging pockets and sacks slung over their shoulders were blocking the way. "Whoa, Storm." Tom eased his horse to a standstill. "What's happening here?"

The tallest man noticed Tom's sword and smiled. "Well, well, a bold, little knight."

An old man came puffing and panting around the corner, pointing a finger at the three men. "Don't let them pass!" he cried, leaning heavily against the wall of a house as he caught his breath. "They're stealing food from the houses!"

"What else can we do?" snapped a small, tubby man, shifting the heavy sack on his shoulder. "We have families to feed."

"This month's supplies never came — you know that!" said the tall, thin man next to him. "We need *something* to eat."

"But those things are not yours to take, Randall!" said the old man sternly. He turned to the short man. "Michael, put them back and take shelter with the others." The three men looked at one another. Their expressions hardened.

"No, Belco, we have to get away!" cried Michael. "How long before the next rockslide flattens the rest of town, too?"

Tom looked at these men. They didn't look like robbers. He saw the desperation in their faces. Thanks to Malvel and the chaos he was causing, good people had to steal just to survive.

Randall bunched his fists and turned to look at Tom. "Get out of our way, boy," he said. "Or you'll live to regret it!"

CHAPTER FIVE

BURIED ALIVE

TOM JUMPED DOWN FROM THE HORSE, TENSING himself for a fight. Elenna stood beside him, readying her bow.

A sudden growling made Tom turn. It was Silver! The wolf bared his teeth as he stalked toward Randall and the others, his fur bristling. Even Tom felt a moment of awe when he saw Silver's glistening fangs.

"A wolf!" cried Belco. "It must have come down from the mountains."

Silver crept toward the men, narrowing his eyes and growling deep in his throat. Randall's eyes grew wide with fear, then he fled with the others, the stolen belongings scattering behind them as they ran.

Belco leaned against a broken wall.

"Good, erm, dog," he whispered to Silver. But Tom could hear the tremble in the man's voice.

"The wolf won't hurt you," Tom told Belco. "He's with us. Are you all right?"

"I'll be okay in a minute," gasped Belco, getting his breath back. "I am the Mayor of Colton. Welcome to my town," he said. A loud crashing echoed through the back alley. There were screams in the distance.

"Another rockslide!" Belco cried out wearily.

Elenna jumped down from Storm. "Hurry!" she said. "I'll catch up with you."

"Come on!" Tom called out to Belco. He helped the old man onto Storm, then jumped up in front of him. There was no time to lose! Tom kicked his heels into Storm's side and they cantered down the alley.

As they turned onto a larger road, Tom brought Storm to a stop. A group of townspeople stood before a crushed home. From inside, they could hear muffled cries for help.

"What happened?" Belco asked someone in the crowd.

"The house collapsed!" said the villager. "Randall, Michael, and Edward are trapped inside."

"Serves them right," said another. "I hear they've been stealing food from the houses."

"Aye, they ought to be left in there to die!" called out a man in the crowd. Others murmured in agreement.

Tom listened as the angry crowd drowned out the cries for help from the trapped men. He had to do something.

"No!" he yelled. The crowd quieted down and

everyone turned to look at him. "We must save these men. It is our duty as citizens of Avantia to help those in need." Tom walked over to the crushed house.

There was a huge pile of stones. Tom could see the rafters of the house poking out at sharp angles between some of the rocks. There was a loud groan as the frame of the house buckled under the weight. They would have to hurry and free the men before the house collapsed further.

"Help us!" came a muffled voice from inside.

"Don't worry!" Tom shouted. "We're going to get you out!"

A sudden screech of anger echoed down from the mountains like a gust of icy wind.

"What was that?" gasped Belco. Tom could guess.

Cypher! he said to himself.

Belco looked away, his face deathly white as another fearful howl tore through the stormy sky.

CHAPTER SIX

DANGER ON THE MOUNTAIN

TOM'S HEART JUMPED AT THE SOUND OF HEAVY footsteps clattering on the cobbles. Eight men stepped toward him. Tom gripped his sword.

"My name is Griffin. We're here to help," the biggest one said. Relief swept over Tom. Then, turning toward the house, he began to think of how to free Randall and his friends.

"We need to know where the door is so we can remove the rocks from in front of it!" Tom yelled to Randall and the others trapped inside. "Can you bang on it for us?"

A faint thumping started up.

The men wasted no time. They braced their

shoulders against the rocks and started to heave them out of the way, but some of the rocks were huge. Even when they used wooden poles as levers, some of the stones were impossible to shift.

Griffin looked up grimly, his hair wet with sweat. "It will take all night to clear this."

"The house could collapse before then!" Tom said desperately. He thought hard. There had to be some other way.

Tom remembered something he had learned in his uncle's blacksmith shop: Everything has a breaking point. One day, his uncle had demonstrated this by shattering a sheet of metal with the soft tap of a hammer. His uncle explained that it was just a matter of finding a point of weakness, and then applying pressure to it.

Tom studied the largest boulder closely. He didn't know what he was looking for until he saw it — a small line near the bottom. It wasn't a crack. It was a line where two different layers of rock met.

Tom pulled his sword out of its scabbard and held it up in front of him. Crouching down, he cocked his sword back, keeping his eyes focused on this small line. With all his strength, Tom swung the sword, striking just to the left of the crack. The impact sent painful vibrations up his arms, but nothing happened to the rock. Tom took aim again and swung the sword even harder.

This time, it hit the mark. There was a sharp cracking sound and the rock crumbled into pieces. Tom could hear gasps of shock from the men behind him.

"What is that sword made of?" someone asked.

"Never mind that," said Tom, examining the next boulder for its weak spot. "We should clear this rubble."

Griffin and the others scrambled to drag away the smaller pieces of rock. Tom kept bringing his sword down in ringing blows against the massive boulders. The muscles in his arms were soon trembling with the effort, but he couldn't stop. Not while people were still trapped in the house.

With a surge of hope, Tom saw the door to the house slowly being revealed. He fell to his knees and used his bare hands to dig away the last of the rubble. The door creaked open. Randall, Michael, and Edward staggered out.

Belco smiled at Tom. "I don't know where you learned to use a sword so well, but that was quick thinking, my young friend." He clapped his hands. "Let's get our new guests to the town hall with everyone else. Come along."

"Thanks, but we'll have to join you later," Tom called, hanging back from the crowd with Elenna. "We can't lose any more time," he added in a low voice. "We must find Cypher and stop him before he can cause another rockslide — or kill someone."

She nodded. "Let's go."

"Hey," said Randall, who was standing with Michael and Edward. Tom and Elenna whirled around — they hadn't heard them approach. He paused. "Not everyone would help to save a thief. Thank you. Are you sure you don't want to take shelter in the town hall?"

"I'm sure," Tom said, with an uneasy glance toward the mountains.

Michael stepped forward. "Are you headed up there?" he asked, alarmed.

Tom nodded solemnly.

The third man, Edward, had been silent so far. But he now looked closely at Tom. "You know, we may be thieves," he said, "but you learn things wandering through the empty side of town."

Tom and Elenna exchanged a glance. "Cypher," Tom whispered.

"Yes," said Randall. "It wasn't always this way — the legends say he protects us! But not now."

"If the giant is what you're after, boy, I'd turn around!" Michael said.

Tom shook his head. "I won't give up," he said.

Edward turned to Tom and Elenna. "If you're set on it, the legends say he lives on a plain called the Place of the Eagles." He paused, thinking. "All the short routes have been blocked. But the main trail will still take you there. It splits in five directions — always take the right. Then an hour's hike will bring you to the plain. That is where you'll find the Beast."

"Thank you," said Tom.

Tom and Elenna climbed astride Storm. With a snort, the horse cantered away, steam puffing from his nostrils. Tom was both afraid and excited as they set off on the winding trail. Looking up at the towering peaks, it was incredible to think of how small they had looked in the distance. The colossal mountains seemed to stretch up as high as the stars, their summits lost in dark wisps of cloud.

The main path twisted and turned up the mountainside, but Storm kept his footing. Rock faces rose up to their right, and to their left cliffs dropped into nothingness. The higher they climbed, the colder the air became. It was thinner, too, and becoming more difficult to breathe.

Finally, the road leveled out onto a plain, where five more paths led in different directions. It was eerily quiet.

Tom pointed. "Randall said to take the right route. . . ."

Elenna frowned. "Looks like Silver wants to take this trail on the left." The wolf was edging along the first path with his head cocked to one side, as if listening to something. Then he started yapping. "What's gotten into you, Silver?" she asked in surprise.

Silver bolted away.

"He must want us to follow him," said Tom. "Maybe he knows where Cypher is!"

Tom urged the horse on. Storm galloped after the wolf. Tom and Elenna leaned forward to take as much of their weight off his back as possible.

Storm was brave and strong, but they both knew it was hard work for him on these steep mountain paths. Elenna looked up ahead and gasped. "Silver, come back!" she yelled. "Now!"

"What is it?" asked Tom.

She pointed upward. "Look!"

Tom felt a chill go through him colder than ice. It looked like a dark cloud was rolling down the mountainside ahead of them. The ground started to shake. Tom could feel the vibrations traveling up his legs. It was like nothing he'd ever felt before — and it wasn't good. Tom knew that was no cloud. It was a rockslide.

CHAPTER SEVEN

THE COMING OF THE BEAST

FOR A SECOND, TOM HESITATED. THERE MIGHT be a chance to get out of the way, but it would mean leaving Silver behind. The wolf could always fend for himself, but before Tom could make a decision, Elenna leaped to the ground.

"There's Silver!" Elenna shouted, pointing as the wolf darted into the mouth of a small cave, half-hidden in the mountainside. "Silver!" she yelled above the gathering roar of the rockslide. "I have to get him," she cried, running toward the cave.

Tom looked up and saw the rocks and debris hurtling down the mountainside toward them.

Silver barked wildly, running back and forth into the cave. The rockslide was almost on top of them!

Elenna reached Silver as the first pieces of rock rained down. Storm reared up, kicking the air.

"We've got to get out of the way!" Tom cried. "Or we're going to be buried alive!"

Tom brought Storm under control and turned him around. He didn't want to abandon Elenna and Silver, but he had a plan. Leaning forward in the saddle, he urged the horse into a gallop down the mountainside. Rocks hurtled through the air.

"Faster, Storm!" Tom urged. "Come on — " He broke off with a cry of pain as a chunk of rock cracked into his shoulder and knocked him off Storm. He felt himself falling through the air. He hit the path with a bone-jarring thud. The pain washed over him, and he could feel himself blacking out. "I have to stay awake," he murmured, forcing his eyes open. But his vision was blurry. He heard the clatter of Storm's hooves disappear into the roar. Without thinking, he rolled over into a small ditch next to the path.

Then the tidal wave of rubble and debris poured past him. His mouth and eyes filled with grit. He squeezed them shut.

Soon, everything went quiet again. For long, silent seconds he didn't dare to open his eyes. When he did, the world was dark and he was covered in the dust and silt thrown up by the rocks that had hurtled past.

Gasping for air, he looked over and saw that Storm, too, was covered in silt, but otherwise unharmed.

"Elenna! Silver!" he called out, straining to hear a response. After a few long seconds, he heard the muffled sound of barking. They were still alive — but the cave was sealed shut by the rockslide.

Tom climbed his way up to the blocked entrance. "Elenna!"

Barely, he could hear her cries for help. He began to scrape away some of the tightly packed dirt.

"Tom! We're trapped!" Elenna yelled out. "We're okay, but I think we're running out of air!"

Tom looked around, his mind racing wildly. He had to free his friends. He began digging frantically at the blocked cave, when all of a sudden, he hit something solid — a boulder. He thought back to the rockslide in Colton. He had to find its weak spot, if it had a weak spot.

"Elenna, don't move. Stay still and breathe slowly," Tom called. "I'm working as fast as I can — "

He broke off as a pounding rumble shook through the ground, soon followed by another and another, each one growing louder and closer.

"Footsteps!" he gasped.

Tom turned around.

A huge, terrifying figure came into sight, feeling his way around a bend in the mountain path. He paused and gave a ground-shaking roar. The whole mountain trembled.

Cypher.

He was as tall as the tallest trees, and his body was more massive than a house. His arms and legs bulged with muscle. His feet left huge indentations in the ground.

He walked like a man, but a man he was not. He was a giant Beast; his gnarled hands ended in yellow claws.

A thick gold collar hung around the Beast's neck. *That must be Malvel's enchantment*, Tom thought. The Beast's mouth gaped open to reveal crooked, yellow teeth. Tom felt fear rising up inside him, pushing the air from his throat.

"Tom!" Elenna yelled. "What's going on out there?"

"Shh!" Tom hissed desperately.

But it was too late. At the sound of Elenna's voice, the giant stiffened. He swung his head slowly in Tom's direction. With another thundering roar, he lumbered toward the cave.

CHAPTER EIGHT

THE IMPOSSIBLE LOCK

THE GIANT TOOK ANOTHER CRASHING STEP toward Tom. He stopped and sniffed the air. Tom stood completely still. The dirt and silt that covered him was helping him blend in.

Tom tried to breathe as quietly as possible so Cypher wouldn't hear him. But there was no way to communicate to Elenna and Silver that they had to be quiet, too.

Silver let out a growl that could be heard even through the blocked cave. Cypher turned at the sound and took another thunderous step closer. Tom didn't dare move. His eyes were level with Cypher's feet. The rough yellow nails were thick with grime. If Cypher took another step, Tom would be crushed. He tried to keep his breathing shallow and quiet, but he could feel his body shaking with tension. He clamped his mouth shut and hoped that his teeth wouldn't start chattering. The Beast swung a heavy fist and let out a roar of frustration.

Cypher gave a loud snort and then let out another roar. He turned and began to stalk his way back up the mountain. Tom felt a rush of relief. The giant had given up! As Cypher lumbered away, Tom saw the clasp that held the collar in place. It gave off a golden glow like Ferno's and Sepron's.

Just when Tom thought he was safe, Silver growled again — more loudly this time. Cypher snapped his head back around, his eye narrowing. He let out a roar and stomped furiously toward the cave. Tom had no choice. He had to distract the giant to save Elenna and Silver. He had to run.

Grabbing the rope and his shield from Storm's

saddlebag, Tom took off running. As he darted through the trees, Tom thought fast. *Somehow I've got to climb higher than Cypher, so I'm level with his neck. Then maybe I can undo the lock and get that enchanted collar off him.*

Weaving through the pines, Tom could hear Cypher coming after him. Each footstep shook the ground. Tom could hear trees snapping and crashing down as the giant knocked them out of his way.

There was no way Tom could outrun the giant — he was too big and too fast. Tom had to buy himself some time.

Scrambling down the slope, Tom spotted a patch of bushes. He made a quick left into the thicket of mountain berries, hoping the bushes would disguise him. He pushed deeper into them. Coming out the other side, there was a huge tree with a hollow in the base of its trunk. Tom dived inside.

The old tree shook with each pounding step of the giant, but inside the trunk it was mossy and soft — and the perfect size for Tom. He tried to calm his breathing and be as still as possible. Tom waited a few seconds before peering out from his hiding spot.

Just a few short yards away, Tom could see the giant's massive legs, the size of tree trunks. *He must be looking around*, Tom thought. Now was his chance. If he could climb to the top of the tree, he might be able to lure Cypher toward him — and get close enough to the lock to free him.

But before Tom had a chance to scale the tree, Cypher began moving. Tom listened as the sound of the giant's footsteps disappeared into the distance.

He had to hurry. Elenna needed his help, but there was no way Tom could save her if Cypher was still on the loose. Tom moved nimbly and quietly, following the thump of Cypher's giant footsteps up the mountainside.

It was hard work climbing up the mountain. With each footstep, loose rocks and pebbles shifted under him, threatening Tom's balance. But he kept climbing until he reached a narrow ridge in the mountainside. Clinging to cracks in the rock, he followed it as it snaked upward to the clouds.

But when Cypher stopped, Tom climbed higher. He hauled himself onto a ledge. Looking down, Tom saw the giant below. Now it was time to free the Beast.

Tom held his breath. The giant was sitting on a wide, flat perch. Above him, a bird gave a harsh cry. Tom glanced up. It was an eagle circling on the currents of air. *This must be the Place of the Eagles,* Tom realized.

Tom lay down flat on the ledge. The stone was hard and cold underneath him but he knew this was his chance. If he edged forward he might just be able to reach the clasp and try to unlock it.

Heart pounding, he edged forward along the ledge until his arms reached the lock. His fingers tingled as they touched the gold. He drew his hand back and grasped for the key around his neck. Then he inserted it into the lock.

Come on, he silently begged the lock. *Unlock.*

Starting to panic, he twisted a little harder.

Too hard.

Cypher suddenly sensed him. With a furious roar, he swung around and lashed out with his huge, clawed hand. It smashed against the side of the mountain, close to where Tom lay. The impact echoed around the mountains. Tom clung to the ledge.

But to his horror, he saw that a crack had appeared in the rock beneath him. Tom watched as the crack zig-zagged its way through the rock.

With a groan, the split widened and the rocks started to crumble apart, dirt and pebbles raining down. Any second now it would give way, and Tom would plunge to his death.

Realizing he had no choice, Tom took a deep breath, scrambled to his feet, and jumped onto Cypher's shoulder to grab hold of the collar.

The giant roared and climbed to his feet. Tom swung through the air, but somehow kept his grip. Cypher swatted at his head with his enormous hands, trying to get at Tom. Tom twisted this way and that, trying to avoid the blows. If so much as a finger landed on him, he would be squashed flat. But he couldn't let go — if he did, he would fall to his death.

Enraged, the giant staggered about, trying to regain his balance. The ledge they were on was narrow and the cracks in the rock made every step dangerous. Tom saw that Cypher was blundering toward the edge of a cliff — beyond it was a sheer drop down into the mist.

With a thunderclap of splitting rock, the ledge gave way. Cypher and Tom plunged into empty space.

CHAPTER NINE

OVER THE EDGE

TOM CLUNG TO THE GIANT, THE WORLD RUSHING by as they fell. For a few seconds they were in freefall. Then Cypher groaned as his back slammed and scraped against the steep slope of the mountainside.

The slope began to level out to a small ledge. The cliff face was steep, but the rough surface of the rock was scattered with ledges and gullies. Tom felt relief flood through him as they landed with a hard thump on a ledge. But they were falling so fast that they skidded straight across the smooth rock. Without time to stop, they went over the edge and were falling again.

The giant tried to thrust his gnarled fingers into some cracks and holes in the mountainside. But he couldn't stop them from falling. Cypher roared and threw back his head.

Tom was shaken free. His fingers closed around thin air as his hands were torn away from the collar. He went hurtling through the air and landed heavily on a steep rocky slope, scrabbling for a handhold. His fingertips dug into a crack in the rock. Terror swept through him as he glanced down. A vast misty chasm was waiting to swallow him below.

This is it, Tom thought, *this is the end!*

To his right, he saw that Cypher had managed to cling on to the edge of the ledge, too. But they were both hanging helplessly.

Tom looked up. He was only an arm's length from the edge of a ledge. But he was barely managing to hold on. His fingers were already numb, his arms tingling fiercely with pins and needles.

Swinging his feet, Tom found a foothold. Then, with the last of his strength, he dragged himself up onto the ledge. Once he reached safety, Tom lay there gasping. Time was running out. He had to get to Elenna before it was too late. But he still had to free Cypher. There might not be another chance.

Tom looked to his left. The giant's fingers were latched onto the edge of a fissure in the rock. Cypher's massive body dangled from the cliff, his feet disappearing into the mist below.

If Tom was ever going to free the Beast, now was the time. He crept on his hands and knees to where the giant's fingers gripped the rock face. Tom was going to have to climb down the Beast's arm in order to reach the lock on the collar.

Tom took his rope and tied one end around a tree root sticking out of a crack in the cliff face. He then tied the other end around his waist. It was now or never.

Creeping slowly, Tom climbed onto the giant's hand and began to shimmy his way down Cypher's enormous arm. Tom felt a burst of warm, wretched air hit him from behind as the Beast let out a ferocious roar. But Tom was safe. So long as Cypher was clinging to the ledge, he wouldn't be able to swat at Tom.

Tom inched his way down until he reached Cypher's massive shoulder. With sure feet, Tom scrambled across his shoulders and to the back of his neck. Holding on to the gold collar for balance, Tom could almost reach the lock.

He shimmied a little further until he was hanging onto the collar with just one arm while he reached for his key with his free hand. If Cypher moved now, Tom would surely fall.

He took a deep breath as he slid the key into the golden lock. With a popping sound, the gears clicked free and the lock opened. The collar loosened. Cypher was free!

CHAPTER TEN

NEW BEGINNINGS

CYPHER LET OUT A ROAR OF RELIEF AS THE collar fell away into the misty depths below. Tom fell along with the collar but stopped with a jerk. His rope held fast.

Dangling above the misty chasm, Tom could see a small ledge just to the left of the giant's knee. He didn't know if the Beast would understand, but he called up to him.

Amazingly, Cypher moved his foot to the ledge. With something to stand on, the giant was able to raise himself up onto the ledge above. With a great struggle, Cypher pulled himself to safety.

From below, Tom watched in awe as the Beast

climbed up the rock face, and disappeared over the ledge. Tom sighed with relief. He had succeeded in his mission. Another Beast was set free from Malvel's evil magic.

Tom's relief didn't last long. With a lurch of his stomach, Tom remembered Elenna. He had to get her out of the cave — and soon.

As he searched for a hold, Tom felt the rope around his waist tighten. Someone was pulling him to safety.

With a final jolt, Tom found himself on the ledge at the feet of the giant. Looking up, he saw a kind expression on the Beast's face. Tom wanted to thank him, but there was no time. He had to rescue Elenna. And, Tom realized, Cypher could help.

Scrambling to his feet, Tom called out to Cypher. "I need your help!"

The Beast let out a booming snort.

"I need to rescue my friend!" Tom cried. "She's stuck in the cave where you first saw me."

Cypher didn't waste a moment. The Beast scooped Tom up in his hand and began moving across the ledge. At its edge was a steep slope that led back down to the cave.

Tom shut his eyes tight as the giant trudged down the mountainside. Cypher's enormous strides brought them down the slope and back to the caves with amazing speed.

"In there!" Tom called out, pointing to the blocked cave. "She's in there." Storm was standing next to the pile of boulders in front of the cave. He had been keeping watch while Tom was gone.

Cypher set Tom down, and with one swift movement of his massive arms, he cleared the debris from the front of the cave. Tom tried to peer in, but couldn't see through the heavy dust that hung in the air.

Then, in a leaping bound, Silver burst from the entrance.

"Silver!" Tom called excitedly. "Where's Elenna?"

Silence hung in the air.

"Here. Over here." Elenna's voice was quiet and scratchy. Tom rushed into the cave. Elenna was slumped in a corner. She looked pale and very tired, but she was still breathing. She had survived.

Tom helped her out of the cave and into the fresh air and mountain sunlight.

"You did it, Tom. You really did it," Elenna gasped as she looked up at the towering giant. "Colton and all the other mountain towns will be safe again."

The color returned quickly to Elenna's face. She sat up to get a better look at Cypher.

"He doesn't look so bad, after all," Elenna said. Tom thought about the chase through the forest, the terrible fall from the cliff, and nearly dropping into a chasm.

"No, not so bad at all," he said with a satisfied

smile. He had survived another chapter of the Beast Quest.

As Tom was thinking about all the adventures he had survived in the last couple of days, he looked up toward Cypher. The giant's single eye welled up with a tear. Tom quickly raised his shield — and the tear splashed upon it. The scorched wood burned bright yellow for a few magical moments. Tom ran his fingers over the surface. It was smooth, as if nothing had happened. With a smile and snort, the giant grunted a farewell and lumbered back into the mountains.

Suddenly, five little wolf cubs came bounding out of the cave! Their coats were white with little smudges of gray around their pricked-up ears and tiny feet. Elenna straightened up and looked at Tom. "This was why Silver ran off in the first place," she said.

"He must have sensed they were in danger," Tom agreed.

"Not anymore," said Elenna, pointing back down the path to where a pure white wolf was hovering. "Look — that must be their mother!"

The cubs jumped about excitedly and bounded off toward her. Silver watched as the mother cuffed and licked them, nudging them together into a group.

"She must have lost them in one of the rockslides," said Elenna, stroking Silver behind the ear. He howled at the mother, who yapped twice, as if in reply. Silver turned and trotted off back down the mountain path.

Tom turned to Elenna. "Come on. Let's follow him."

Tom and Elenna made their way back down the path to Colton. Tom led Storm, who followed quietly.

They made the journey back as quickly as their aching muscles allowed. To their surprise, a group of townspeople were waiting near the town hall.

"We heard another rockslide and worried you two were caught in it," Belco said, sighing with relief.

Tom and Elenna just grinned in response.

"We don't have much, but we'd be happy to share." Belco went on. "Won't you join us in the town hall?"

"I have a feeling we will have to move on soon," Tom told him. "But thank you all the same."

Belco nodded. "Well, if you change your mind, you're always welcome," he told them, and turned to go back inside.

"Whatever path you take, may it bring you fortune," said Randall grandly, before ducking into the town hall with the others.

Tom and Elenna shared a glance, then they grabbed each other's hands and swung around in a dance.

"We did it!" cried Tom. Now that the danger was over he felt overwhelmed by both exhaustion and relief.

"We did!" agreed Elenna, gasping with laughter. As they swung around and around, a figure appeared before them. They stumbled dizzily to a halt. It was the wizard!

"Aduro!" Tom breathed.

"Congratulations, my young friends," Aduro told them. "I have been watching your progress from the king's castle."

"We've freed the third Beast," Tom told him proudly.

"And you have received Cypher's enchanted teardrop for your shield," Aduro observed. "It will give you magical protection. Should you ever find yourself plunging from a great height, hold the shield above your head and it will slow your fall."

Tom looked at his shield. "Fantastic!"

"You have done well," Aduro told them. "But the greatest dangers still lie ahead. Will you continue with your Quest?"

Storm chose that moment to whinny, and Silver barked in response. Elenna beamed at them both.

Tom nodded firmly. "We will see this Quest through to the end."

Aduro smiled. "Then travel on to the plains at the center of the kingdom," he told them. "Tagus the Night Horse awaits you there."

"We will find him," said Tom. "And whatever harm he's doing, we'll stop it."

"Good luck," the wizard said, as his image faded away to nothing.

"Do we have to go right now?" Elenna wondered, smoothing her hair from her forehead. "A warm dinner sounds good. We haven't had a meal in a long time."

Tom's stomach growled at the thought of food. In the distance, he could hear voices and the tolling of the town bells as Colton slowly returned to life.

"Maybe we should stay here for just one more night," he decided. "I have a feeling Aduro is right. The biggest challenges lie ahead — and we'll need all our strength to meet them."

They stood there silently for a moment, Storm and Silver by their side. Elenna turned to Tom, and he smiled at her.

Whatever dangers lay ahead, they would face them together.